Emmy
the Exaggerating Elephant

Fenton
the Fearful Frog

Gertie
the Grungy Goat

Herbie
the Happy Hamster

Ivy
the Impatient Iguana

Ollie
the Obedient Ostrich

Perry
the Polite Porcupine

Queenie
the Quiet Quail

Rupert
the Resourceful Rhinoceros

Wendy
the Wise Woodchuck

Xavier
the X-ploring Xenops

Yori
the Yucky Yak

Ziggy
the Zippy Zebra

D0492703

NOTE TO PARENTS

Albert's Special Day
A story about friendship

In this story, Albert the Absent-minded Alligator remembers that it's a special day — but he can't remember why. His absent-mindedness gets him into one predicament after another until, with some help from his AlphaPet friends, he finally discovers what makes this day special indeed.

In addition to enjoying this delightful story with your child, you can use it to teach a gentle lesson about the important value of friendship — of being a good friend and having friends.

You can also use this story to introduce the letter **A**. As you read about Albert the Absent-minded Alligator, ask your child to listen for all the **A** words and point to the objects whose names begin with **A**. When you've finished reading the story, your child will enjoy doing the activity at the end of the book.

The AlphaPets™ characters were conceived and created by Ruth Lerner Perle.
Characters interpreted and designed by Deborah Colvin Borgo.
Cover design by the Antler & Baldwin Design Group.
Book design and production by Publishers' Graphics, Inc.
Logo design by Deborah Colvin Borgo and Nancy S. Norton.

Albert's Special Day

RUTH LERNER PERLE

Illustrated by Deborah Colvin Borgo

Grolier Enterprises Inc.   Danbury, Connecticut

Albert the Absent-minded Alligator was fast asleep. Suddenly, *Rringg....rringgg...rringgg!!* The alarm clock woke him up.

Albert turned on the radio. "It's going to be a sunny day, folks," announced the *AlphaPet News* reporter, "just the right kind of weather for this very special day."

Albert turned off the radio and sat up in bed. He scratched his head.

"Hmm, a special day," sighed Albert. "There's a string on my finger and an arrow on the calendar. That's to remind me that today is a special day. But what's so special about it?"

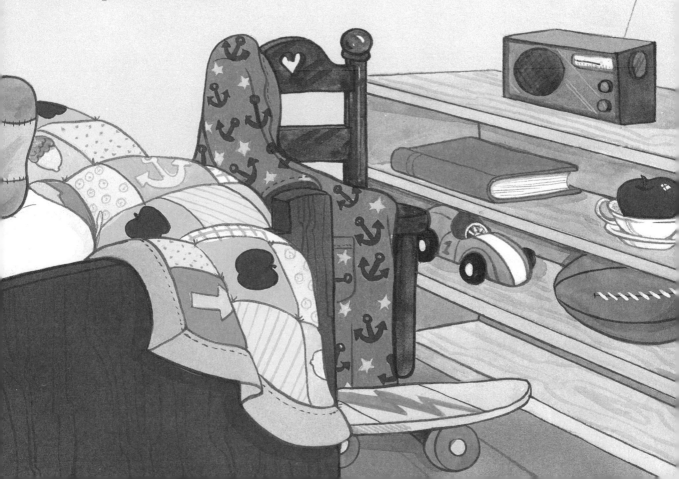

Albert muttered to himself, "A special day, a special day, why is this a special day? And where are my glasses? I can't remember where I left my glasses."

Albert got out of bed and reached for his blue bathrobe covered all over with little red anchors.

He put one arm in one sleeve. Then he put the other arm in the other sleeve. But something wasn't right.

Albert looked down at his robe.

"Oh dear, what happened to the buttons? And where are the pockets?" he wondered. "There's something wrong with this robe."

Albert took off the robe and dropped it on the floor.

"Well," thought Albert, "if this is a special day, maybe I'd better take a special bath."

He went into the bathroom and turned on the cold water. He turned on the hot water. Then he looked for the drainplug. And that's when he saw his peanut butter and jelly sandwich in the soap dish.

"Well, well, well, there it is! I've been looking for that sandwich for the longest time!" cried Albert. "Now if I could only remember where I put the plug, and my glasses! And if I only knew why today is so special!"

Albert looked everywhere until he finally found the plug. It was inside his cup with the little angel painted on it.

He put the plug in the drain and made sure it was tight. Then he poured in a cup of pink bubble-bath.

"This will be a special bath for a special day," said Albert, "whatever that special day may be."

Albert was about to step into the water when the telephone rang. He hurried out into the hall to answer it.

"Hello! Hello!" said Albert. But all he heard was a funny squeaking sound: *ggreeelymung!*

Albert was holding the telephone receiver upside down.

"This is all happening because I can't remember where I put my glasses!" grumbled Albert.

He turned the receiver right side up.

"Hello, hello! Can you hear me, Albert?" It was Emmy the Exaggerating Elephant.

"I just called to tell you I'm busy, busy, busy getting ready for this most special day. I'm so excited I can hardly wait! Yippeee!"

Before Albert could say a word, Emmy hung up.

Then, Perry the Polite Porcupine called.

"Good morning Albert," he said. "We're all making preparations for today. I'm calling to remind you not to forget to say hello to all your friends. And be sure you thank everyone on this special day. Good-bye for now."

As soon as Perry hung up,
Katy the Kind Koala telephoned.

She said, "Dearest Albert,
today is such a special day.
Please let me know if there is
anything I can do to help.
And please try not to forget to
look your very, very best."

"Oh, yes," answered Albert,
"I was about to take a bubble
bath and..."

Just then Albert heard the
sound of water gurgling.

"The bath water!" cried Albert.

He dropped the phone and ran
toward the bathroom.

In the bathroom, all Albert could see was bubbles, bubbles, and more bubbles.

"The bathtub! Where is the bathtub?" he cried.

Then he heard a *splish*

and a *splash*

and a mighty *whoosh*.

Water was pouring over the edge of the tub. It swept across the floor, and knocked Albert down.

PLOP! Albert landed on his rubber duck and went sliding out the bathroom door. The bubbly water swooshed him across the landing and toward the stairs.

There were mountains of bubbles everywhere.

The water rushed all the way down the stairs and into the hall. And Albert went bouncing down with it.

He saw his sandwich sailing by, and his shoe and sock, the angel cup, his toothbrush, the soap, washcloth, and sponge.

The water crashed against the screen door and pushed it open.

Albert whooshed out the door and bumped down the front steps.

Bump,

bump,

bumpety,

bump,

bump.

That did it! His glasses slid down his forehead and settled on his nose.

"My glasses! I found my glasses! This *is* a special day!" he cried.

And that's when Albert saw all his AlphaPet friends.

Everyone was smiling. The water made great puddles around their ankles but they didn't mind.

"I'll run in and turn off the water," said Bradley the Brave Bear.

Emmy carried a big cake decorated with candy apples, apricots and almonds. Everybody held packages and presents.

HAPPY BIRTHDAY

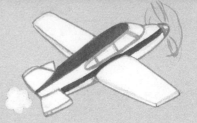

Albert heard a whirring sound overhead.

He looked up.

An airplane was writing a message in big, puffy letters. It said **HAPPY BIRTHDAY.**

In the yard, a table was set with food and party hats. And there were all kinds of games to play. There were jump ropes, bows and arrows, balls, and even a trampoline!

Hanging between the apple tree and the oak tree was a big banner that said **HAPPY BIRTHDAY, ALBERT!**

"Oh, it's my birthday! How could I forget that?" said Albert with a great big smile. The AlphaPets laughed. "Yes, it is your birthday, Albert," they cried. "It's your special day, you absent-minded alligator!"

HAPPY BIRTHDAY, ALBERT!

"Help me remember my favorite words."

anchor

acorn

ax

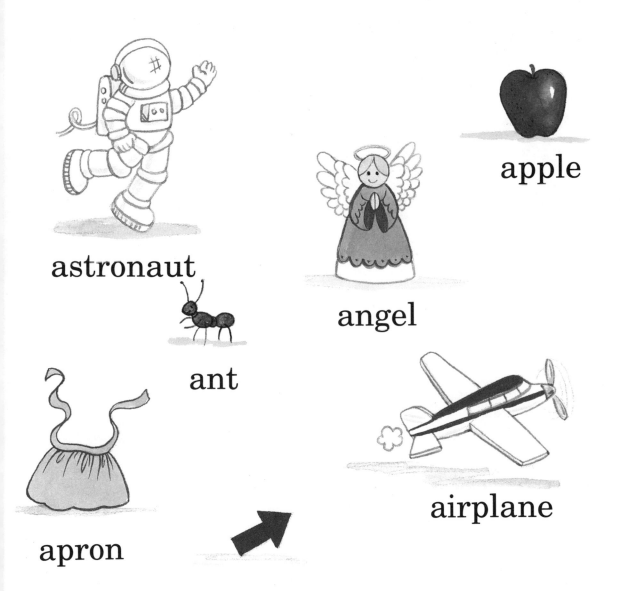

astronaut

ant

angel

apple

apron

arrow

airplane

Look back at the pictures in this book and
try to find these and other things that
begin with the letter A.

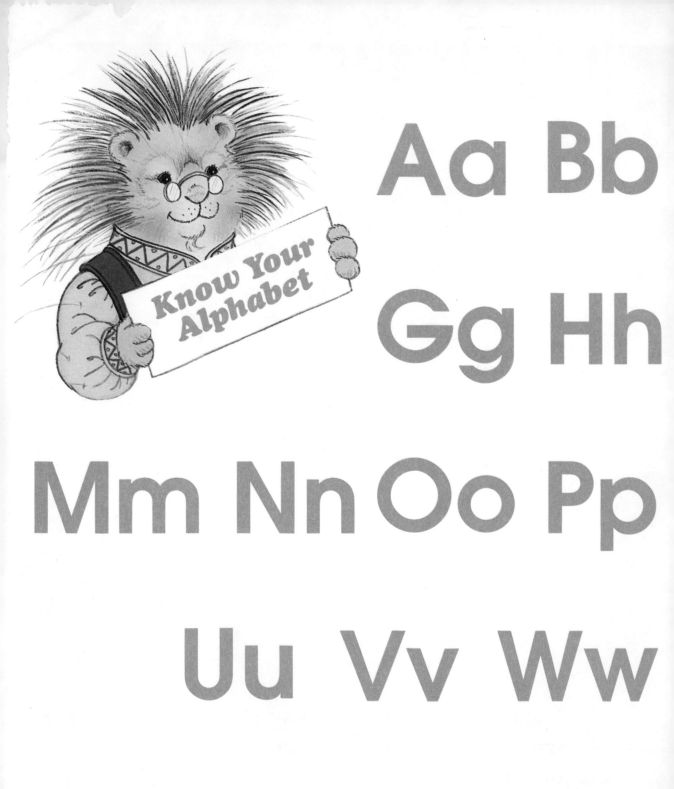

Aa Bb

Gg Hh

Mm Nn Oo Pp

Uu Vv Ww